JEFFREY AND HIS BUNNY

To order additional copies of this book, contact:
Xlibris
844-714-8691
www.Xlibris.com
Orders@Xlibris.com

ISBN: Softcover   978-1-6641-2644-2
          EBook   978-1-6641-2643-5

Print information available on the last page

Rev. date: 08/15/2020

JEFFREY AND HIS BUNNY

By: Peggy Sue La Croix

Once upon a time, there was a little boy named Jeffrey who lived out in the country. He loved to go berry picking in the summer. He lived with his mommy and daddy. His mommy Milly was a stay-at-home mom and his daddy Fred was a truck driver who was gone a lot!

As his daddy pulls out of the driveway in his semi and waves goodbye, Jeffrey yells "Goodbye!"

His mommy was hanging clothes up on the line.

Jeffrey said, "Mommy, I'm going to go for a walk in the trail

and pick some berries. I'll be back soon."

"OK, don't go too far, son. You're only seven," his mother said.

So off Jeffrey went down the trail, when all of a sudden, he saw something.

He bent down and saw a whole bunch of bunnies!

So he slowly and quietly got down on his hand and knees,

snuck up on one, and lunged out and grabbed it, holding so tightly!

So happy and so excited, he turned and ran back for home.
The bunny wiggled and squirmed and tried to get away. Jeffrey
just held on tighter as soon as his mother was in sight.

"Mommy! Mommy! Look! Look! I've got a bunny.

Can I keep it, Mommy? Please?" Jeffrey yelled with so much excitement!

"Look at my new pet!"

"Well, Jeffrey, owning a pet is a lot of responsibility.

You have to feed it, water it, and clean out their cage too!"

"I will, Mommy," said Jeffrey,

"so I can keep the bunny! YES!"

"Yes! You can have your bunny!"

"Thanks, Mommy!"

And off he went to the garage to get a cage, got the bunny some carrots and cabbage, and got a bowl for water. Then he took the bunny in the cage to his room.

Jeffrey started hearing crying!

"It's the bunny crying!" Jeffrey said.

"Why are you crying?

I'm going to take good care of you. You're going to be my pet!"

The bunny cried louder!

"I want my mommy! I miss my mommy!" said the bunny.

"Oh wow! You can talk?" Jeffrey said.

Soon it was getting late. Jeffrey was getting tired.

The bunny was still crying at the end of his bed in the cage.

"Please let me go," said the bunny.

Jeffrey tells the bunny, "You're going to like it here, you'll see!"

While the bunny still cried for his mommy, Jeffrey
put his pajamas on and got into bed.

Mommy Bunny was looking for her baby. She called out, "Lucky!

Where are you, Lucky?"

And Lucky could hear his mommy calling for him,
but he could not get out of the cage.

His mommy couldn't hear him as well.

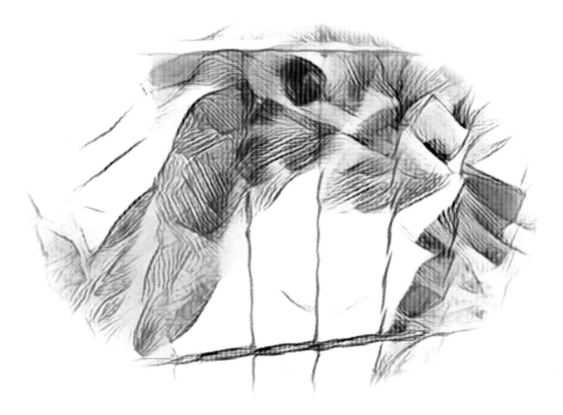

Outside the window, Big Daddy Bunny was yelling for
Lucky too. Lucky was still crying and scared.

Jeffrey, on the other hand, had drifted off into a
deep sleep and woke up in Bunny Land.

"Where am I?"

As he looked around, all he could see were bunnies and
tunnels all around. Jeffrey was scared and crying. He asked the
biggest bunny, "How can I find my way back home?"

The bunny replied, "I'm Jonny, the big daddy around here, and I don't know where your home is!"

"My home is here under the ground," Big Daddy said.

"This is our bunny woods, and we don't leave unless

we need to find food or the family goes to play."

So confused, Jeffrey cried, "I want my mommy!"

A very nice bunny came over to greet Jeffrey.

"Now dear, dear, I bet your mommy does miss you. I'm Esther, queen of Bunny Land,

and I'm a mommy too, so I would surely miss my son if he wasn't here."

"What does your mommy look like?" said Esther Bunny.

"My mommy is beautiful, and she has blond hair,
and she loves me very much," Jeffrey said.

"And how did you get here?" said Esther.

"I don't know!" Jeffrey cried.

"I need to find my way back home."

Jumping down out of a hole was a little bunny.

"I'll help you," said the bunny.

"How can I help you?"

"Who are you?" said Jeffrey.

"I'm Lucky," the bunny said.

Jeffrey said, "I'm looking for my mommy, and
I need to find my way back home."

"Yes, I'm lucky, and I'm lucky to have my mommy too—just kidding!

Come on, we'll look in the holes that leads to the tunnels
back up to the clover trails," Lucky the Bunny said.

"I can't fit in that hole!" said Jeffrey.

"Well, let's go to the hole my grandpa uses."

Then Jeffrey started to cry again, yelling out, "I want my Mommy! I don't know how I got lost."

Then he tried to fit through the tunnel. He got stuck and fell down. As he started screaming and falling, he woke up on the floor beside his bed.

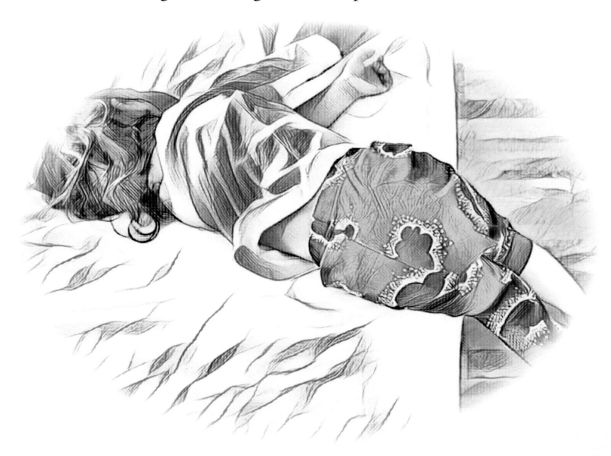

"Oh no! Oh no! What a scary dream!" Jeffrey said.

The bunny still sniffling. Then Jeffrey knew what he had to do.

He went over to the cage and told the bunny,

"I'm going to call you Lucky because I'm going to take you to your mommy."

"How did you know what my name is?" said the bunny.

"I didn't know your name. It came to me in my dream," said Jeffrey.

"I heard my mommy calling me while you were
sleeping. I know she's looking for me.

Big Daddy too. I was crying, but I couldn't get to them," Lucky said.

"First thing tomorrow morning, I'm taking you home," Jeffrey said.

"Did you hear me crying and telling you my name
and my mommy's name was Esther?

I'll be so glad to see her and hug her so tight. I
know she misses me and is very worried."

"Your mommy's name is Esther? Are you kidding me? That's
what her name was in my dream. Everything you are saying
came in my dream. I suppose you have a big daddy too?"

"Yes! That's my grandpa's nickname. When one of us is
missing, it's his mission to find us. I was yelling at you when
you were sleeping that Big Daddy will find me."

"Well, that's the craziest thing I've ever heard, but you sure taught
me a lesson. I was scared and missed my mommy so much. You've
got to miss yours! We'll find your mommy," Jeffrey said.

"Really?" said Lucky.

"Really!" Jeffrey said.

"My dream made me realize how much I love my mommy,

and I would hate it if anyone took her away from me.

Come on, let's get you out of that cage. Get up here
in my bed until morning," Jeffrey said.

Early the next morning, Jeffrey went down to kitchen and squeezed
his mom real tight and said, "Mommy, I love you, but I've something
I must do! I'll be back real soon. I'm taking the bunny home!"

So Jeffrey took Lucky, and down the trail they went. Guess who he saw . . . Big Daddy!

Grandpa was calling for Lucky! "Grandpa! Grandpa! Here I am!"

"Where have you been, Lucky? We've been worried sick about you!"

"That's my fault, sir," Jeffrey said.

"Excuse me, but who are you?" Big Daddy said.

"I'm Jeffrey! I caught Lucky on the trail yesterday!"

"You did what?" Big Daddy said.

"Lucky, what did I teach you about strangers?"

"I didn't leave! I love my mommy!"

Then Jeffrey spoke up. "Please, sir, Big Daddy, I'm sorry. I took him to my house, and I wanted to keep him and make him my very own pet and friend forever. I didn't realize I was hurting him, taking him away from his family. Even though we're not alike, our hearts are the same.

I'm very sorry, sir," Jeffrey said. "He loves his mommy like I do."

"Well, why wouldn't he?" Big Daddy said.

"I get lonely. I don't have friends or sisters and brothers," Jeffrey said.

"But when I realized he needed his mommy as much as
I do. I knew I had to take him back home."

Out behind a bush, jumping with joy, came Esther,
Mommy Bunny, hugging Lucky oh so tight!

She was crying and telling him how worried she was
about not being able to find her baby.

Lucky was crying happy tears. "I missed you so much!" Lucky said.

Mommy Bunny Esther put her hands on her hips, and told
Jeffrey, "That's my little boy, and when someone messes
with him, they've messed with the whole family!"

Jeffrey said, "I'm sorry! I never wanted to hurt him. I just wanted
him to be all mine. I guess I was being selfish and not thinking
of anyone's feelings but mine. But now I know I was wrong."

"Well, I'm afraid sorry is not good enough," Esther Queen Bunny angrily said.

"We can't find Holly now, Lucky's little sister.
She was trying to find Lucky too!"

"Jeffrey, she went looking for her brother when you took Lucky, and now she's missing. We've looked everywhere but haven't seen her since. This is your fault, Jeffrey!" said Esther.

"Please! Please! Let me help you find her," Jeffrey said.

"OK! We need all the help we can get. Holly is in danger!" said Esther Bunny.

Everyone was calling out and looking for Holly when Jeffrey said, "Quiet! Listen!" He could hear her calling out for help. "I found her!" Jeffrey said. "She's trapped in this pickers called a burdock. I can get them off her."

"Thank you! Thank you, Jeffrey!" said Esther.

Esther hopped over to hug her baby Holly with
happy tears when she was found.

Holly then hopped over and gave her brother Lucky a hug and said,

"We might fight now and then, but I would miss
you forever if you weren't around!"

Holly thanked Jeffrey for bringing her brother back
and saving her from all the pickers.

They all agreed to be friends and playmates forever, but not in the same home.

Big Daddy thanked Jeffrey for bringing Lucky home and helping to find Holly.

Lucky rounded up the whole crew, and Mommy Esther and
everyone greeted Jeffrey with kindness, for Lucky had a safe
return. Lucky and Jeffrey would now be best friends for life!

Every time Jeffrey went berry picking, they played on the trail and had fun!

Jeffrey said, "It's so much more fun to just be friends!"

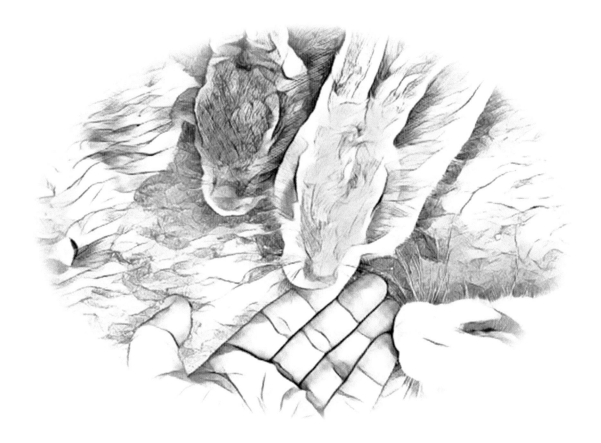

Lucky bounced with joy with the freedom in his own world,
and together with his family and with pride and joy, he
introduced his other brothers and sisters to Jeffrey.

"You helped save Holly, so now you can meet my sisters Jasmine and Annie
and Logan, Patrick, Mason, and Wesley, my brothers, so they can race
through the trail and stop and enjoy the sweet taste of berries along the way."

Then Jeffrey went home and explained what happened to his bunny to his mommy. He then told her about his dream. Jeffrey's mommy was so proud of him for doing the right thing. She gave him the biggest hug.

Jeffrey and his mommy left carrots and lettuce on the trail so the whole bunny family could enjoy food and fun with family. They all were jumping with laughter and having fun.

Mrs. Milly and Mrs. Esther greeted each other and became friends.

While all the bunny family was out to play, they took time for a picnic and enjoyed all the sweet berries they'd gathered in the fields. Together they put strawberries, raspberries, blueberries in one basket. Oh what a feast they had!

Then they all hopped and skipped down the trail.

Bunnies were all around, and a happy little boy,
Jeffrey, made many new friends in one day!

Jeffrey and Lucky would forever be best friends because they
learned how important their mommies were to them and knew
how important it was to respect others' feelings now.

What a surprise!

Lucky went to see Jeffrey in the winter, and Jeffrey gave him carrots and goodies to take back to his family. Jeffrey loved to see Lucky and hugged him before he left!

So they both lived happily ever after, best friends forever!

Oh the love in life with friendship.

THE END

Hello! I'm Peggy Sue LaCroix. This is the second children's book I have published. I have also written a poetry book called Peggy's Poetry & Song Lyrics. My passion is to write. I've lived here in Attica, Michigan, for thirty-seven years, filled with love for my children (who are now all grown) and grandchildren. I now have four monkeys (which are my wild babies :)), five Pomeranians, and five mini horses.

Printed in the United States
By Bookmasters